The
Reluctant
Dragon

Retold by Lesley Sims

Illustrated by Fred Blunt

Aaargh!

One summer's evening,
a shepherd tore down the hill to
his cottage. "**Aaargh!**" he screamed.

He flung open the door.

"I... just... saw... a... dragon," he panted.

"A **dragon?**"

shrieked his wife.

"A **dragon!**" thought their son, Sam.

"I wonder if he's friendly?"

The next morning, Sam set off to find out.

"I'll be extra careful,"
he promised his parents.
"At the first sign of smoke, I'll run!"

But the dragon **was** friendly – and he was thrilled to see Sam.

"I love my cave, but it does get lonely," he said.

The dragon told tales of long, long ago.

Once upon a time,
fire-breathing dragons
filled the skies.

They kidnapped princesses
and battled bold knights.

The dragon loved telling stories
and Sam loved hearing them.
Every day, he came back for more, until...

...the villagers found out about the dragon. They were terrified. They trembled in their tunics and quaked in their boots.

We need someone to fight this monster!

SLAY THE DRAGON!

BAN THE DRAGON

BANISH THE DRAGON!

NO DRAGON

FIGHT THE DRAGON

SLAY THE DRAGON!

Sam raced off to warn him.

"The villagers want to get rid of you!" he gasped. "They say you're **dangerous**."

Nonsense! I wouldn't hurt a fly!

That afternoon, Sam
heard even worse news.

Look! It's Saint
George, the
dragon killer!

Oh no!

Hurray!

Sam rushed back to the dragon.

"Saint George has come to fight you," Sam shouted.
"And he has the longest, **pointiest** spear I've ever seen."

"But I don't like fighting," said
the dragon. "I'll hide in my
cave until he goes."

"You can't," said Sam. "He'll find you."

The dragon yawned. "I'm sure you'll think of something," he drawled.

Sam wandered through the village square,
thinking hard.

A crowd was telling Saint George
about the dastardly dragon.

When the villagers had gone, Sam went up to Saint George.
"It's not true!" he protested. "The dragon wouldn't hurt a fly."

"But they want me to fight
him," said Saint George.
"What can I do?"

"I've got an idea," Sam said.

"Come and meet the dragon."

"Here's the plan," said Sam.
"You could have a pretend fight."

"But it must look real," insisted Saint George.

And then we can
have a feast!

Mmm...

The next day, Sam waited nervously
by the dragon's cave.

The entire village
trekked up the hill
to watch the fight.

Colossal cheers broke out when Saint George rode into view.

But **where** was the dragon?

A roar echoed around the hills.
Flames blistered the air
and the dragon
thundered out of his cave.

"**Charge!**" yelled Saint
George, galloping forward.

The dragon bounded up...

...and they shot past
each other, with a wink.

"Missed!"
cried the crowd.

Saint George and the
dragon swung around and
charged again.

CLATTER! BANG! OUF!

The dragon gave a groan and slumped
to the ground. Saint George stood
over him in triumph.

Cut off
his head!

Spear
him!

"I think the dragon has learned
his lesson," declared Saint George.
"Let's invite him to our feast."

And he led the villagers,
Sam and the dragon
down the hill.

The feast went on until the stars came out – and everyone was happy.

Sam was happy because his plan had worked.

The villagers were happy because they'd seen a fight.

Saint George was happy because he'd won.

But the dragon was happiest of all,
for he had lots of new friends...

...and a very full tummy.

The **Reluctant Dragon** was first published over 100 years ago.
The author was Kenneth Grahame, who also wrote the famous
children's story **The Wind in the Willows.**

Designed by Caroline Spatz
Edited by Jenny Tyler

This edition first published in 2013 by Usborne Publishing Ltd., Usborne House, 83-85 Saffron Hill, London EC1N 8RT,
England. www.usborne.com
Copyright © 2013, 2009 Usborne Publishing Ltd.